Dandelions & Dragonfly Wings

J. W. Shane

Plans

I know that look
Eyes gazing into mine like a child's
Subtle biting of the lips and the
> slow
> sensual
> swallowing after each
> sip of her merlot

Fingers unconsciously exploring the stem of her glass
Indeed, she has an interesting evening planned for me

Cloud

Pillows
Blankets
Everything soft
The afternoon daylight pouring through the windows

She lies there smiling
Waiting for me
Inviting me
I lie alongside the comforting warmth that radiates from her

Her skin so pleasant to the touch
Arms entangled
I feel her heat engulf me
My mouth then placed where neck and shoulders meet

Deep breaths brush against my ear
Wrapped in her and
Everything soft
We become a light cloud of bliss

Wide

These sheets, this skin
Long for the warmth of your body
These hands hunger to grip your hair
Teeth that wish to hold the skin of your neck
Fingernails hoping to be riddled with the skin of
       your backside
Grabbing it hard, spreading it wide
Pushing you down, pushing me inside

This nose wants nothing more than to be filled with the
       scent of our sex
These arms desire to hold you down, unable to break free
Cheeks whose sole concern is to have upon them your
       labored breath
As you shudder, gasp, and fall across me like death

Disappear

Stand against me
Let me wrap my arms around you
Disappear in my embrace
Vanish from the sight of the world and
     for the moment
        be only mine

Signature

Smiling when looking into the eyes of friends
Slightly blushing in the presence of family

The flooding of memories brought about by the constant
        nagging tenderness of where I have marked her

Thinking of me each time she sits, a little softer than usual

How I owned every single inch of her

Putting her flesh through unknown and
        delightful uses
Leaving my signature behind in the form of
        bite marks and bruises

My Sky

Stand above me
Pour your liquid over my being
Let it run across my outstretched limbs
May it flow to the ground where gravity drags it
      through the soil to my roots
            nourishing me
                  keeping me safe and well
                        conditioning my chlorophyll
So that I might properly utilize your light
To grow strong and rigid for the purposes that you
      would have me fulfill
For you are my sky and
      I will grow toward you until the day I die

Eclipse

Corrupting your heart
      as the eruption of my love meets your lips
Darkening the sun
      as the moon hides its light with an eclipse

Rain

To make love in the midst of a summer's rain
The growing heaviness of our sopping hair
Cool droplets washing away the day's sweltering heat
    from our faces
The ground dampening the way she does
    for me
Wet clothing peeled off like a second skin
Exposing our naked bodies to the delightful tapping
    of heaven's release
As we release ourselves
    into and on each other

Patience

To drag a rose down her uncovered spine
Slowly
Steadily
Cultivating tiny erections across her skin
      as if they were reaching out to me
Wanting so much more than the delicate sensations
      currently being offered
More will simply have to wait
Patience, my dear
Patience

Darling

I long for someone who loves that I call her "darling" as I pull back on fistfuls of hair

Phases

How cruel is the divide of time that celestial entities must
    also beckon?
Waning longs for waxing but both never in the sky together
    to provide light for the shadows of the souls
    autonomously strolling below

Meeting in secret
Only cloaked in the darkness of the new can they share
    with one another out of the sight of those who wish to
    map their phases

Intertwined, unknown by all

But oh, the thrashing of the salinous liquid tide they cause to
    spill upon the shore

Guiding

I love the guiding of her hands
    holding my palm up to her heart
I feel her soul, her pulse, her life
    I can't stand to be apart

I love the guiding of my hands
    placing them where my eyes can't see
So warm, so soft, so wet, so deep
    she's taking all control from me

Lavender

With the slowest of movements
She takes the lace adorned, lavender panties
        from around her hips
                to her knees
                        to her ankles
                                to the floor
She presents herself and I make use of the velveteen
        dessert she has prepared for me
As if she knew that this was why

        I merely picked through my dinner

Light

Despite my operation of the switch the room remains black
"I've removed them."
I hear her voice from the corner
She approaches me with well-adjusted eyes,
        lowering me to the floor
Lying back, I close my eyes despite the
        encapsulating darkness
Listening, the sound of a foot softly landing on the floor
        is heard by each ear
Blood rushes through me in a frenzy as her warmth settles
        upon my lips
"I've brought you into the dark so that I might be your light."
Is whispered by a voice so soft I swear I'm hearing it for
        the very first time
"Taste, and see how brightly you make me shine."

Right Above Me

Taking me on her back she reaches into the nightstand
        producing a bottle
With a sparkle in her eye and a sly grin on her lips, she pushes
        forcing my withdrawal
Using the contents, polishing me to a beautiful shine
Guiding me to the destination she has chosen
Applying pressure, I enter her
Slowly
        to the hilt
Holding ever still, watching her eyes
Her body accepts me, allowing me to take form
Plunging into the intensely hot, smooth, slippery wrapping
        that surrounds me
Using delicate fingers, another is filled
Right above me
Feeling everything through the thin tissue that separates us
Eyes close and that unmistakeable wrinkling appears on her
        forehead and cheeks
I know that look
It appears each time she begins to melt all over me

Any Second

Placing herself inside of him
Wide-eyed and surrounded by warmth
She moves with the careful cunning of a
      lioness
Knowing that her mate could pounce at
      any second
She manipulates what makes him a man
Forcing eruptions from within
Leaving him weaker than any prey he has ever
      licked his lips at with hunger

Umbrella

Clouds
Cool air
Visible breaths
Raindrops
Splattering footsteps
Warm lips
Soft tongue

Shared umbrella

Undone

Our eyes met with enough ferocity to cause the epicenter
of our souls to climax
before the first button
had been undone

Everything

I ache for an adventurous lover
Seizing every opportunity
A lover who, like me, longs to
See
Smell
Hear
Touch and
Taste
Absolutely everything
No harbored inhibitions
Giving ourselves to each other completely

Ravens

When I see her, ravens fill my soul
No light emits to frighten my demons
      into hiding
Lust and pure human desire
To become her through the heat of her
      frenzied riding

Bathwater

In front of me she sits in my open lap
    facing away
Up to her mid-torso in warm, calm water
As the sponge is gently squeezed between my hands at the
    top of her shoulders
I watch droplets draft tributaries along the fair glow
    of her skin
Leaning forward to provide kisses that allow me to sample
    the sweetness of skin-tinged water

How her wet skin shimmers in this light
The way the dry, slightly frazzled hair on the top of her head
    cascades down to a plethora of points wet with
        bathwater

Reaching around her jawline I tilt her chin,
    pouring warmth from her forehead back to dampen
        the remainder of dry hair
I shampoo her
Fingers fully enthralled in discovering each rise and fall
    of her scalp

Suddenly she stands and turns towards me
The petals of skin that make her a woman at eye level

She sits

Her knees at my hips

Warm breasts held against my chest as dripping arms
        wrap around my shoulders
She looks down as I rinse the foam from her hair
When finished, she looks up at me with hair
        sticking to the side of her face
Those eyes
I see my soul in each iris
        and I am afraid
Terrified I'll open my eyes and wake from this reverie
Having read my eyes she forces her lips to mine
        holding the back of my head
            keeping my lips against hers with wet hands
                in my hair
Taking my fear and assuring me that
        this is no dream

Possession

There is no angel in me
The purpose of my soul is simply to
>   take possession of your body

Butterflies

Fingers slowly brush the hair from your face
Eyes that bring confessions from your lips
Arms that wrap around so warm
Your heart can't calm its pounding skips

Kisses flood your neck and shoulders
Moving down you get no rest
Placing lips on open, bare skin
Like butterflies landing on your chest

Savor

To taste a woman
The pliable skin of her nipples
Elastic wrappings of her womanhood abiding the contour
        of my lips
I wish to use my mouth on even the most secret
        of places
Bringing her to life on the breadth of my tongue

Cacao

With greedy fingers and thumbnails I pry her layered covering
     away from her to reveal the treasure kept hidden
        from me
Safe from the potential afflictions brought upon by exposure to
     the ambient air

There she is

Glowing with a satin reflection of the light around us
A matte tapestry that was truly made for only my mouth
Bringing her close I inhale,
     dragging her scent through the subfloor of my senses
Placing her to my slowly parting lips
I close my eyes
     I nibble
       I bite and
         I taste
Gently forcing her across my tongue
She melts and permeates every taste bud as I repeat
     until she is no more—dissolved, swallowed
Leaving me with a smile and her lingering flavor
     long after she is gone
The memory of how she felt against my lips and on my tongue
     permanently imprinted on my soul

Sand

She loves to walk barefoot in the sand
The crushing of grains beneath her feet provide her with
        memories of a younger version of herself
           and an even younger lover
Making love in the sand
Toes and knees digging ever deeper
Scent of salt in the air
Climaxes producing droplets that fall from her
      bestowing to the beach a small taste of their
        passion

Stardust

Leave the light on so that I might gaze upon
    the most gorgeous thing stardust has ever assembled

Teacher

I used my hands
    lips
    teeth
    tongue and
    cock
To answer questions she hadn't realized her body
    was dying to ask

Again

Her lips would never beg, but
      the wavering of her breath
      the fixating of her eyes
      the licking of her lips
Silently scream that she's willing to give everything
Just to feel me
      inside of her again

Grabbing

With my face buried where a shoulder meets your neck
      I slide a hand up your gooseflesh riddled spine
              to unclasp
Grabbing skin with my teeth
The flesh of a breast that seems to leap into my grip
"Fuck!" jumps past your lips
      as I lift from behind
Exploring underneath your dress

In My Absence

All I want is to be touching
        your skin in my presence
Being the inspiration for your dirtiest thoughts
        in my absence

When

Was it the way he licked his lips before he spoke?
Was it the cold gaze of his icy blue eyes?
Was it the black and grey stubble that peppered his jawline?
She hadn't settled on "why"
      she was just deciding "when"

Angel

Descend upon me my liquid angel
    wrap me in your velvet wings
Caress me
      from my beginning to my end until
          warm confessions flow from me and
         hold me until I sleep

World

What I wouldn't give for her to place her hands
      between her legs
Opening herself up for me
Exhaling heavily as I present an open-mouthed kiss to the
      world she has revealed

As the Storms

They had made love in and as the storms of summer so that
     even in November
She fights the urge to close her eyes
     drop her jaw
          and touch herself at the sound of thunder

Always Warmer

I'm always warmer
    with you on my mind
When thinking of you
    heat runs over me like liquid
Gathering in places that
    inspire self gratification

Gentleman

She proclaims that I am quite the gentleman after I
　　　open the door and allow her to ascend the stairs
　　　　　　before me
What I'm thinking about doing
　　　to what I am seeing
Characterizes me as anything but

From the Inside

There was something she loved about being naked
      while he was clothed
Straddling his lap
Wrapping her arms around his shoulders
Laying a breast in his mouth and
      soaking the outside of his pants
As his helplessly restrained cock dampened them
      from the inside

Hush

These fingers long to taste the delicacy that is your skin
To place a traceable memory across your being the way
      an introspective stroll leaves footprints in the
          warmest of sands
Collectively they breach the most secret of pathways
      as a single finger lays across murmuring lips to whisper
      "Hush."

Dreams

Stumbling upon him soundly sleeping
She enters the room like a kitten
      ready to play
Slowly
Carefully
She draws back the sheets
Taking him into her mouth to see if she appears in his
      dreams

Sacrament

Part your lips
    allow your eyes to close and
        lay your head back
So that I may fill your chalice with the blessed sacrament
    that bestows your wicked soul with salvation
For what I provide is truly the Lord's supper

So Sweet

The porch light is off
The final open sack has received its bounty
Smiling as I walk with the bowl of unclaimed prizes
        eventually dispersing them on the bed

Playfully we open piece after piece
Tearing the wrappers with each other's teeth before
        shamelessly devouring each delectable morsel
Opened wrappers litter the bed like leaves on an
        October afternoon
Brushing my hands through the piles of paper and plastic
        attempting to find my next sugary victim

But I am left finding nothing

Looking up, I find her smiling, holding the final treat
        in open hands—a piece of red licorice
I make a motion demanding it be delivered into my palm
        but someone insists we share

Placing it between her teeth, I join her at its opposite end
Our lips meet as we take bites from our respective sides
        while holding it in place with closed mouths
After the inaugural severing, I taste her breath
        traveling through its hollow core

A reverse nod of her head removes it from my mouth
        allowing her to chew it to bits in front of me
        while curving lips form that fucking sly grin of hers
I pounce, push her back and kiss using my tongue to forcefully
        pry her lips apart and retrieve any crumbs of sweetness
                I can
She giggles in a display of victory before I straddle her waist
        reach down and close my hands
With a single motion I rip open her top as the buttons that
        once held it across her torso are strewn
        throughout the room
She gasps with a mixture of shock and agitation while
        attempting to push me back and pull my shirt
        over my head
Failing from the lack of mobility awarded by my knees holding
        her blouse to the bed below
Deciding to help her I finish the removal of my shirt before
        hopping off the side of the bed

She attempts to sit up, but a quick push to the center of the chest
with my open palm returns her back to the bedspread
        before I grab the waistband of her pants with both
        hands
She howls with laughter as my fingertips push against her
stomach
        dragging fingernails against skin before settling
        behind the single button
It releases with a near silent "pop" while the zipper is opened
        with each tooth making a soft click in its
        last attempt to keep her covered

"Well, well, well."

45

It's at this point I discover that no panties obscure her
    from my sight
Just her gorgeous, pale skin glowing in the light
Her eyes sparkle as she removes each leg from the cotton
    they had once resided in
The fabric hits the floor at the same time my knees drop
        to the carpet between the feet that were dangling from
        the side of the bed
My lips meet her with a softness that grows into a
    frenzied abandon

Her fingers run through my hair while mine enter, the rocking
        of her body allows her clitoris to dance
        across my tongue
Warm, smooth, and viscous as I drag my fingers through her
This is the candy I've truly craved
Suckling, tasting and exploratory probing give way to a release
        of air from her lungs and a pooling of pleasure around
        my hands provides effortless movement as fingers
        explore the soft, warm, wet and pillowy landscape
        kept from light and the sight of men

Sitting, our mouths meet as she eagerly accepts the taste that
        permeates my mouth and is the reward of my labor
The blending of flavorful remnants of cherry candy and the
        fruits of her quaking linger among us while the
        topography of our wet mouths refuse to release
        from one another

My hands rest on her thighs as she throws her arms back
        flinging her now useless clothing onto the littered
        duvet

Mouths still holding together as she reaches back to release
	the hooks and loops keeping her breasts covered
	before tossing the bra behind her to land on the floor

Arms are lowered around my shoulders as a pert nipple is
	taken into my mouth
Holding me against her with little room for respiration
Pushing her down with her breast in my mouth, raised legs
	are pulled to the edge of the mattress
A belt is unbuckled
	trousers are dropped and socks are removed
	before placing my feet back to the floor, only to find
	candy wrappers keeping portions from making
	contact with the carpet

Her hands reach and lather me with saliva before pulling
	me to meet her
I glide in effortlessly until a single step is necessary to
	remain perpendicular
The heat from inside her feels nearly hot enough to burn me

The first stroke is slow
Deliberate time is taken while her eyes are held with mine
	and her mouth slowly opens
	granting permission
The fucking is hard, forcing expressions of approval
	in the form of closed eyes, lifted eyebrows
	biting lips, monotone groans and
	nipples reddening between her pale fingertips
I release while holding against her as tightly
	as possible
Her lips slowly crawl into a soft smile as she feels throbbing
	and a foreign pulse beating within

I fall to my knees to taste the cream filled confection I have
      made of her

She sits and helps me to my feet, wrapping arms around me as
      my flaccid penis is held against her chest
The bliss of the moment interrupted by the sensation of hair
      being pulled out of my thigh from the removal of paper
      that had adhered to me at some point

Observation leads to the discovery of bodies riddled with
      candy wrappers
As each is removed skin is tasted to enjoy the
      mingling of flavors embraced by these tongues for
      the first time
She drops to her knees removing another from a leg before
      taking my pitiful form into her mouth
Slowly sucking, I am released from her lips before she
      makes eye contact
            smiles and softly says
               "Si charmant!"

Peel

I climb atop the sheets she uses to
      cover herself
Such a thin barrier between our bodies
Saturating the fabric with an eager mouth
I peel the covering from her to devour
      the sweetest of fruits kept hidden
          under the rind

Phase to Phase

The moon has always meant more to me
    than the sun
She loves for me to gaze upon her beauty as her amorous
    dance leads from phase to phase
She adores being the light in my darkness
While the sun has only offered blindness and burns

Quiet House

Stars and moon hang in the sky and
      silence fills my home
It's good to sit and think of things
      when I get time to be alone

No movement from anyone else here
      so full of peace between the seams
Knowing that my children sleep
      I imagine what they see in their dreams

Appliances cycle and my ears slightly ring
      hearing the sounds of eyelids as I blink
Swallowing noises, pulse is loud
      a droplet rings out as it hits the sink

Traffic slows as the moon drops low
      she and her horizon soon will meet
Stretches, thoughts, and drawn out yawns
      might be telling me it's time to sleep

End of the Day

She dips into a warm bath at the
        end of the day
Lies back and lets the hot liquid permeate her skin
Wrapping her in a fluid embrace all her own
No need to share
No need to think
No need to prove anything to anyone
Just be there for and to take care of herself
To soothe her busy mind
Relax and melt
If just for a moment

Sea to the Sand

Window open on a still evening
I lay in bed
Wrapped in plush warmth
On my side, near fetal with
    blankets tucked under my chin
Unseasonably mild air fills my lungs while the sound of
    highway traffic outside constantly ebbs and flows
        like waves gently lapping at the shore
The hours climb and the tide pulls the swells further out to sea
    bringing silence throughout the room
This silence stays until the sunrise kisses the atmosphere
    with blue
        and the Earth's tenants bring the sea to the sand
      once again

Silence

Sometimes silence is my savior
It's a wonderful feeling to be alone with my thoughts
Reflection
Introspection
Scenarios and
Memories
Giving myself a moment to
Hope
Wish
Dream
All the things I love for a second into being

Ever Will

I love an unmade bed

Morning hair, sleepy eyes, and big yawns

Deep stretches, sticky tongues, thirsty mouths, groggy minds

Having as much of the day as you ever will

Sunday

Relax
Recharge and
      rest
For tomorrow is that fucker known as Monday

Fail

The absence of light seems to amplify
      the sound of my mind
As realistic thoughts fail in their attempts to strong-arm
      my whimsical musings into submission

Evenings to Come

Cicadas abuzz
The aroma of manicured lawns
Humidity of the season and the tackiness it applies
      to your skin
Tangerine skyline giving way to the evening's embrace
Torches and candles add a flickering light that brings the
      flight and feast of bats into view
The cool flavor of fermented perfection swirling on
      on your tongue
The remnants of ethyl lingering with each
      closed mouth exhale

Summer dreams inspired by the ground being
      blanketed in snow
         this close to spring

Wishing Well

Shimmering reflections of a starlit sky
Sent into motion when
     metal meets moisture

Cascading ripples full of dreams delightfully meander
     in every direction
The way children run through school doors to the playground
     on the first warm day after winter

Stillness filled with
     "could have beens"
          altered by faithful waves of
              "please, let it be"
As eyes are closed
     breath is held
          coins are tossed and
              desires are placed in the hands of hope

Fire In the Sky

Through the night awake
    trading toil and frustration for currency
On occasion, happily ending my day by filling each eye
When beauty takes the form of
    fire in the eastern sky

Overshadow

My mind is set that the joy of desires I have will always
overshadow any sadness

Little Something

Holding doors
Writing notes
Making small gifts
Leaving change in the vending machine
Smiling
Saying "thank you"
Using terms of endearment

You never know when a weary soul is silently begging for
        a little something to brighten their day

Winter Wind

I love to hear the wind
Especially in winter
The rustling of barren tree limbs
The silence of the season
The cold embrace of chilled arms
Her voice in my ear, insisting that I
"Shhhhhhhhhh"
That I only need to hear her

Orchid

I affix my lips as silently as the fog appears on a
      warm winter morning
Placing kisses at her navel
Moving down slowly, the same way nectar drips from the
      pistil of an orchid
I will feast on her
      because I am starving and
          she has every intention
              of keeping me alive

Discovery

Europe
The Mediterranean
Smell of salt and olive groves in the air
Everything new to the both of them
Falling in love
Discovery
One day at a time
Laughter
Lingering eye contact

Penance

You're my sinner and
      only I may grant you redemption
Indulgences are unnecessary
The penance I require
      will indeed bring heaven to you

Masterpiece

Stillness around
Quiet chill of the air we breathe
Loneliness between us
Remove your garments so that I may see your nakedness
       bathed in the winter moonlight
The emerging topography of your flesh casts
       thousands of tiny shadows
The reddening of your skin transforming you into my lavender
       masterpiece under the cascading starlight
The standing hairs give the contour of your body a rebirth
I baptize you in the warmth of my touch
Causing long cold embers inside of you
       to glow red with desire

Manners

When I am buried within while pulling handfuls of hair
        expletives,
        "yes"
        "please" and
        "thank you"
                are the only words I want from your mouth

Our Sins

How I want to awaken next to you
Running my hands along the skin of your back
Finding you tacky with the evaporated sweat of the
      night before
Taking in the sight of the remains of pleasure-forced tears
      collected like dust around closed eyes
To slide my naked legs across bedsheets still
      slightly damp with the release of
          our sins

Petals

She spreads her legs
        for him
As the dew-laced petals of morning open themselves
        for hummingbirds

Conclusion

Eyes close and an open mouth smiles as I taste the conclusion
   I've brought upon her skin

Play Date

I place used fingers
    at your lips
Inviting you to taste the demons you've brought for me to
    play with

As She Walks

Wind rolling the fog across the landscape
    the way her skirt flows as she walks
The day brightening with the lifting of either

Words

The only words I want you to say are to be spoken as moans
placed into my open mouth

Fluid

Reaching down to wash her feet
A fire is sparked by the heat of the water cascading between
      her spread buttocks
Reaching back to the valve, she commands more
      fire from the falling fluid
Heat that permeates her, leaving her with no choice but to
Close her eyes
Clutch
Grope
Explore
Prod
Causing her to create liquid herself

Watching

I pour myself a drink
Sit down in the most comfortable of seats
Relaxing, I gaze at her from across a sunlight-filled room
     as she hovers over him
Eventually taking sight of her lowering onto my friend's
     waiting body
He glistens
With every rise and fall
She looks back at me with playful eyes
As I take a sip, savor, swallow, and eventually lick my lips
Holding eye contact with her as she fucks him
He seems slightly unsure
     but I have plans
When finished with her
Her mouth will be mine and her ass is to follow
I will fuck her while his untouched remnants flow
     from her body
Until she physically can take no more

But until then, I shall drink
Drink and observe

She looks back at me again
Smiling, biting her bottom lip
I'm in heaven knowing that ass is soon to be mine
And oh, how I love watching it work
From here

Winter Solstice

Night begins to fall on a cold December evening
You flip the duvet
Inviting me with a smile and a curling finger
Wrapping the sheets around us
Looking into each other's eyes
Hands exploring, unseen beneath the bedding
Warm
Damp
Smooth
Hardening places
Gripping
Feeling
Sense of touch like fire
Wrapping your legs, pushing me to my back
Settling upon me
Exhaling as we interlock
Beginning our first of many sessions
Exhaustion being our goal on this
      the longest night of the year

Redefine

Winks
Half smiles
Shifting in your seat
Eyes
Visage
Take my hand and redefine the taste of sin with me

Shiver

Lady Luna rises and casts her glow
　　　on everything below
The heat of the sun is gone, forcing
　　　lovers to hold each other to stay warm
Kept apart by the light of the day
　　　they keep each other close, lest they shiver
　　　from being alone
They see themselves differently in the moonlight
　　　away from the judgmental shine of diurnal existence
Secrets revealed
Only visible under this minimal brightness
Only seen with the touch of a cold hand under a sweater
　　　to a warm, soft back
Felt like a chilly nose-to-nose greeting
Sealed with eye contact
　　　and a smile

Her Turn

She sits on the sofa next to me, covered to her chin in
      blanket
A sly look overtakes her innocent face
I deduct by the smirk and the movement of the covering
      that she is touching herself
        out of my sight

Her flushed face gives way to an open mouth and
      heavier breathing
An erratic movement drops the blanket
      nearly exposing a breast
I reach over to return the fabric behind her neck

The is not for my eyes

She whispers something so softly it is rendered inaudible
Motions slowly subside
A glistening hand is presented to me from under the covers
      allowing me to taste her fingertips

Revealing a reddened cloak of skin she tosses the blanket
      onto my lap
Insisting that it's her turn

Similar Softness

She loves park benches
       cool mornings and
            hot coffee
Enjoying the three, a single leaf falls upon
       her lap
Rousing memories of the night before
When his lips
       touched her there with a
            similar softness

True Deliverance

Pressing me against the wall she kneels
Forcing exposure of the epicenter of my
      shame

At first I cannot look
Sensations of pressure and heat as
      dampness envelops me

She releases a muffled sigh
A sound with which I am unfamiliar
I shudder, frightened and invigorated

Her intent is evident
She wishes to drink from me
To ingest the suppressed wanton I've kept inside

She gives, giving as she also takes
Draining from me the inhibitions from the very depths
      of everything I've ever kept hidden

A tremendous weight is lifted from my soul
My being becomes weak and warm
A blissful triggering like I've never known

I open my eyes afraid of what I might see
Lowering my chin to my chest I see her

Those dark eyes full of happiness knowing that she
        has released me from my chains
Saved me with true deliverance

I was set free behind the threshold of her smile

She stands
        holding her cheek to mine
Whispering into my ear that everything is
        going to be fine

Shatter

There was something about the way the window frames
cast shadows over her clothing barren body
on bright sunny days
that made him want to shatter her
like panes of glass

Towel

Entering my presence the towel is dropped
      at her feet
Settling upon my lap she drags the tips of her freshly showered
      hair across my open mouth
A warm, damp breast is fed to me and upon the initial
      tooth-laden gripping of her nipple
      a heavy sigh exits her lungs
          and lands joyously
             upon my ears
The perfumed aroma of her freshly bathed skin
Her back warm and soft
Buttocks newly cooled with exposure to the ambient air
Reaching around her to explore the destination of my
      choosing
Every morning should begin with this

Cat Nap

Awakened from my afternoon nap by the placement of
    warm skin across my back
Draping her nakedness over my shirtless body she
    kisses the back of my neck and whispers
        "I need you to hold still."
Closing my eyes to feel her move
    hands are forced between my abdomen and the bed
Pants are unbuttoned and pulled mid-thigh with a strength
    I didn't know she had
Straddling me, I feel her heat make contact with my
    lower back
Feeling hardened nipples meet my skin quickens my pulse
She pushes
    grinds and
        drags her clitoris across my flesh
Making motions that eventually become as fluid as the desire
    she coats me with
Pushing my erection painfully into the bedsheets
    the pressure becoming strangely enjoyable
More weight is pushed against me, movements become faster
    I know this rhythm
    I know what she's up to
The pelvic rocking becomes more erratic
    legato to staccato

Unmistakable breathing that leads to a humming in my ear
    a gasp
           and finally a puddle that forms
               between our bodies

Soft Awakening

Entering the room as she dreams
She startles slightly as I caress the
       back of her neck
Sleepily groaning
Hands working past the shoulders
Down the spine
Past the tailbone
Giving flanks a firm squeeze
Kneading the muscles of her back
       like a baker perfecting a confection
Up to the shoulders
Once again sliding down her spine
Further
Up
Over
Down
In between
Under to where a slightly surprising dampness envelops my
       fingers with a quivering warmth
Extracting incomprehensible whisperings from her lips

Polka Dots

Failing to find a route to break away
     my mind from these delicious thoughts
There's little I can do to resist
     against pierced nipples and polka dots

Sonnets

Her arms around my neck
    my hands in her hair
Legs clutching me as I pull the skin of her shoulder
    with my teeth
Music playing loud enough to drown every sound

Someone could have been outside
    but who really knows
We were too busy
    writing sonnets in the fog on the windows

Honey

Dripping onto me with the movement of
a hives's most cherished honey
Adding sweetness to my bitter skin

Afterthought

On her knees she waits, palms on her thighs
I approach and slap her hands away as she reaches to
      unbuckle my belt
Rules state that she isn't allowed to place her hands
      on my belt
I open it for her
      allowing her the button and zipper

Dropping my garments mid-thigh she releases me

Gazing upon me like a starving animal,
      she softly takes me into her mouth
Warmth and pressure triggering a pituitary overload
Blood gathers from all corners of my being
I run my fingers through her hair, eventually
      gripping and
            pulling her head back and
                 dropping to her level
                     tasting myself on her tongue
I give her mouth a playful slap and place hands
      around her throat
            gently forcing her back to meet the floor

Lifting a leg, I nibble from her ankle along the
      center of her calf
            kissing the back of her knee

Gently biting the inside of her thigh produces howls of
        tickle-roused laughter
I move further until I meet her center
There she greets me as if a warm pastry had been placed
        at my lips
                smooth and sweet
                        melting across my tongue
Rising to my knees I force her to turn face down
Grabbing her hips with determined hands
        dragging her to me until her backside is upright
All is open and inviting
I devour everything within my reach
        savoring inside and out
Moving up, I place my blood filled display of desire
        along her precious folds of skin
Hungrily she rocks back and forth across the top of me
        until my desire cannot be calmed

Pushing down on her lower back forces her glory to
        formally present itself
Holding myself at her dampened opening
        coating myself with her invitation before
                easily sliding ever so slowly
                        until our bodies completely interlock

As we manipulate each other my hands are kept busy
Striking
        gripping
                pinkening her pale ass
                        pulling firmly grasped fistfuls of hair

She quakes around me

The monotone symphony from between her lips
        becoming louder and louder
Finishing with quiet gasps and soft vocalizations
Staying still until she is silent before disconnecting from her

Applying liquid to my hand I massage around the smallest
        of her openings
Entering slowly with one finger, then another
Gently pushing
        pulling
            twisting my wrist
                carefully spreading fingers inside of her

Placing myself where my fingers meet my palm
        I push myself in while withdrawing them
            placing myself where the two once were
Gliding in up to the hilt
Holding still to feel her tensing around me
Her body subsides it's movement granting me
        permission to move
The silky smooth feeling on the inside of her body
The groaning from deep within her throat and the
        pressure from her fingers being placed where I was
            moments before
Send me into the familiar throes of release with no
        hope of return
Growing weak I empty myself inside of her

My body softening, withdrawing from hers
        without my will
I collapse at her side with heavy breaths and sweaty skin
Reaching under her arm to cup and caress an exposed breast
        rolling the nipple between tired fingertips

Kissing behind her ears
For a moment our once labored breathing slows
     matching one another's
I close my eyes
   exhale
       and feel a small amount of liquid push itself
       from my well-worked penis
"An afterthought" I giggle
She reaches back, easily collecting it with a single finger
     moving to place it in her open mouth
A glistening tongue meets the remainder of my emission
She tastes
   coyly smiles
       and proclaims that she likes the way I think

Welcome Home

Kneeling before her as she sits
      sliding the shoes from her tired feet
Running dedicated hands across and around them
Applying and releasing pressure in an effort to deliver her
      from the tension of her day
As my hands work around her achilles
      ascending a delicate leg
Leaning down to me our foreheads meet and hold together
Minutes of closed eye silence pass, broken by a whisper
      under my breath
"Welcome home. How I've missed you today."

Fear of Thunder

Daylight lasts longer
Sunset lingering on the horizon later and later into the evening
Hope of warmer days
      unspoken in the hearts of some
The underlying fear of thunder beneath the skin of others

Brothers

A cricket chirps in desperation among the glitter of
     frost upon the grass
Orion, winter's guardian, sits high in the southern sky,
     ignoring his cries
I feel as if we were brothers

Among Them

My heart was pieced together along the multitude
    of galaxies
Assembled from the colliding of lovelorn celestial bodies
Resulting in a kinship with the stars
Knowing that I am meant to be among them

Can Never Exist

Perceptions of warmth in objects
      we know to be cold
Why do we find so much beauty in things that
      we know we can never hold

I sit under the moon and feel Lady Luna's
      arms across the abyss
Begging for life to enter a world
      that can never exist

Marionettes

We are never truly ours
The heart pulls the strings of our lives
      as though we were marionettes
Never fully allowed to touch the ground
      despite our dreams of standing

Void

I am currently a void
Nothing but an empty vessel
Scaled through and through by the residuals of loneliness
        and guilt
Empty
Barren
So much that from these blinks nothing falls
        from the hurt under these eyes
Out of desperation what they can produce
        falls from wet lashes like dead flies

Translation

The heart feels in a language
Tongues can't speak
Much as eyes scream in cries
Ears will never hear

Tide

Words aren't always available
    to express a change of heart
No person truly knows you, although they may claim
    otherwise
All change as does the love you have for them
Ebbs and flows of the heart are expected
So then why are we forced into guilt
When your moon doesn't pull the way it once did
And the tide drifts away
    never to return

Bright

Bright, warm sunshine
My eyes inhale emotions through color
Yellow, red, green
Radiant are the autumn leaves
As was that one Christmas Eve
The light long missed in my
       grandmother's eyes
Why is everything so beautiful before it dies?

Lost

Feeling so strange
That I just don't know
How can I be sitting in my house
      and still want to go home?

Someday

Standing alone
Artificial rain falling over me
Heavily exhaling I ask too many questions
    "What the fuck am I doing?"
    "Is this everything there is?"
Reaching behind me I turn the valve
Taking away the cold added for comfort
Too much—just stay and adapt
Questions flow as my skin turns red
Closed fists impact my chest to distract myself from the
    pain on my skin
The thought of "someday" gives me the strength to stop
    the water
Despite my heart wanting to self-destruct

Take

Drink and cry
Tell me your biggest fears
What caused you to shed the heaviest of tears
Be honest
Be brazen
Unapologetic and angry
In this moment consider no one but yourself
         because this is your time to grieve
No one gets to take it from you

Where She Is

To sit behind her
Running my hands up her neck
Massaging the base of her scalp
Easing her tension
Taking her thoughts from her surroundings until she eases
Relaxes
Falls back to my chest where I can wrap my arms around her
Holding her where I am,
Not where she is

Snowflake

To fall like a snowflake
     into the river
Become one with what she is
A portion of something big
An object of importance
To drift to the bottom and for once be feasted upon

Devour

The water doesn't reflect the way I wish
        that it would
The more you smile the more distorted and refracted your
        reflection becomes

My beauty is not seen by the surface
True internal beauty is a nonessential trait
We are visual beings
Our eyes persuade our hearts to negate what is truly needed

So many more beautiful than I but dark of the soul
Will have the possessions my heart desires
This is the world
Hearts beckon to the will of the eyes

I could fill an ocean with what I feel I have to offer
The sweetest fermented fruit remains in the wine skins
Letting its intoxicating fluid slowly
Evaporate over time

I will wait
Drowning in my own naïveté, thinking that mine will
        eventually be recognized
Until then, I wander next to this river while the beautiful
        devour

Crushing

The crushing awakening that comes in knowing
      you'll never be able to truly look upon your sun
      with the eyes you wish to give it

Swear

I'd swear I hold you in my dreams
Always inside you when I sleep
I wake up desperate and alone
With no one laying next to me

The world doesn't accept me like you do
The weight that's off of my heart
I know it's not to be
We will always be apart

I can't help it, I think of you all the day
The world around me, cold is all I feel
I hear your voice and read your words
Single-sided wish that it was real

Frozen

I love her when she's restrained
Hardened
Petrified
Where the ice is thin I can see her eyes
That's all I need
Those I read
They speak to me when lips are unable to
I use my hands
An effort to crack the frozen surface
To release the fluid turmoil she keeps for me underneath
I know it's there beneath the frost
Ready to pull me under
I wish to bring this out of her
In her rushing undertow I wish to drown

Say

Waiting to hear more
Impossibility grows every day
Pried apart heart all tattered and torn
I still hang on all the words that you say

See Her

Jealous, yes I am
Of what their eyes have had
No matter what their visions were
They'll never see her like I have

In Dreams

Someone will get to touch you there
While they're down upon their knees
Gently tasting what you have
He'll get to leave you pleased
Scent and sight and fingertips
Will give you what you need
But this happens for me
Only inside my dreams

Miles Away

Stillness all around as I walk
Silence of the pre-dawn
Each cumulus reflects the high pressure sodium glow
      of the city that they blanket

Many are still in slumber
Meanwhile, I awake with thoughts of my lover
Causing visions of an unseen and unconscious beauty to
      meander through my mind

Oh to see her, to fill my nose with the raw scent
      of her body as she drifts from dream to dream
To inhale the air from under blankets as she shifts to her side
      pulling covers up to her chin

To be the first thing she sees at daybreak
Opening her sleepy eyes to a blue room full of sunrise
To be the "good morning" she reciprocates
      as she sits
          groans and
              stretches

But I am miles away

Pilgrimage

I await her words with the same fervor with which Mary took
      her hair to Jesus' feet
Surely it was not only the mane in her hands that was
      permeated with adoration for him

Sitting in the place our second cerebral encounter began,
      I bathe in the morning sun
Smiling as the droppings of autumn's grip playfully tumble
      past my feet

To this place I will make my pilgrimage

Glimpses

Eyes welling from the glimpses of beauty my eyes were
      blessed with on the eve before
Hair unraveled
A glow radiating from her skin
Pinpoints of ornamental melanin scattered across her face
      like stars in the night sky
Bold, dark eyes presenting a myriad of depths I long to explore
Presented in a frame of vulnerability that will be
      forever on my mind

Sharing a Drink

I'd love to look into your eyes from across the table
Take in your smile as you laugh
Sharing a drink
Reliving days gone by
> anecdotes and stories
> mistakes and accomplishments
> celebrations and regrets

Revealing who each of us truly are
Developing a genuine trust and friendship
Something that we can keep with each other
Occasionally being reminded at later times when the coolness
> of the glass we drink from meets our lips

Different Season

In a place that is sacred to me
The same leaves on the ground
      only in a further state of decay
Familiar breeze carrying the scent of a different season
      still stirring feelings and memories
Restraint not fleeting this time
Calm and quiet
Keeping to myself
As my mind goes there once again

Taking Steps

Afraid of putting the candle to the fuse
Tired of being nothing so I will try to be something
Taking steps
Moving pawns
Finished gathering webs on an old forgotten shelf
The world won't take a chance on me so I'm taking one
      on my fucking self

Metamorphosis

Hardening layers of a past life
Becoming something new
Opening myriads of faceted new eyes
The world is seen as something different with my
          newfound ability to fly
It doesn't matter what has triggered this
Splitting pain down my back
I'm leaving my exuviae
Completing my metamorphosis

Static

Static in the skies
      causing pain into my eyes
Fog of apprehension
      distorting this connection
Strain of parted years
      blaring in my ears
Definition gone from my sight
      everything taken by the light

Cold

The warmth of summer cannot keep my soul's breath from
appearing as fog

Words and Silence

Sometimes it's taxing to be equally in love with both
words and silence

First Taste

Warm winter days are the simplest of
    blessings
A tiny embrace of warmth that covers the body in the delight
    of the impending spring
As the first taste of chocolate delights a child

Twinkle

The air pulls a fog from my lips
Cold and brisk to the eyes and nose
Myself and everything around me preparing for the inevitable
        freezing to come
The suspension of life
But oh, do I ever adore the way the stars twinkle in winter

Shush Now

It hurts
When someone I love is in pain
I want to take it
To hold, shush, and rock her like a child until she slips into a
       dream where things aren't so real
To let her tears soak my chest
So I can lay her weary head on her pillow and try to give her
       grief some rest

Both

Kind words have never been easy to ingest
A lifetime of subpar choices and personal disappointment
     keep me painfully more than humble
Locked inside myself
Alone
Feeling worthwhile and beautiful have never graced me
     but for a second
     for the first time
I felt like I was both

Clarity

My mind is ever restless
A firework that never stops exploding
Filling the sky with flames
Obscuring the stars with smoke
Filling every ear with a persistent, percussive pounding
Multitudes of onlookers awaiting a pause
       that never comes
Fire growing ever larger
Sulfur-laced fog growing more and more dense
Blackened, suffocated vision and blinding fire
      consuming all
Until clarity is but a memory, a wish

During the Day

When the faded moon is visible
within the azure mixed with gray
The night reassures that she still holds me
even during the day

Forever Grey

When the sun shines after so many
  cloudy days
The sky embracing you in its firm arms of
  light and warmth
The brightness parading across your face like the hands
  of a long absent lover
Whispering in your ear that a new day will come
And that your skies will never be
  forever grey

Hope

I still wish on falling stars
      birthday candles and
            blown dandelions
And find luck in coins found on the ground
I say "hello" to each skipper that flutters across my path
Finding delight in the territorial chasing of dragonflies
The world to me is one of wonder and beauty
She always will be
      every day that I open my eyes

The Child Inside

Never lose the child inside yourself
Find shapes in clouds
Go down slides
Hold an insect
Think about why things are
Play in the rain
Watch a meteor shower and wish on every streak
Build a snowman
Cuddle during a thunderstorm
Go fishing
Write a note
Climb a tree
Sing out loud to your favorite song
Color
Draw
Build a fort
Rekindle the childish curiosity you gave up in your
      adolescence
Leaving our wonder behind is the cruelest thing that we
      ever do

Sky

It's everywhere
All around us
Giving us the stars required for late night wishes
     and clouds to characterize during the day
Citrusy sunrises
Tangerine sunsets
Plum twilight
I get lost in the sky
We can find something wonderful around us, any time of day
     if we'd only look up

In Her Slumber

Only the sound of breath breezing through your sleeping nose
Restless am I
Tireless I am
To wonder what you dream

Thin strands of hair drape across your tired face
Hidden irises swimming under closed eyelids
Incomprehensible mumbling spoken through immobile lips
      that I hope are speaking my name in her slumber

Good Morning

The blue of first light envelops the room
I open my eyes to find hers gazing at mine
Frazzled hair
Freckled nose
The scent of rested breath
A small peck of her lips is placed on my forehead before
       she whispers "Good morning."
Half of the day is spent wrapped in smooth bedsheets and a
.   heavy duvet
Heads sideways on pillows as we converse about life
While the snow outside the window kisses the ground

Hair

Lay your head on my chest, darling
I wish to breathe the scent of your hair
Run my fingers through
Bring handfuls up to touch my face
Dig through it deeply
Wrap your scalp with my grip
To massage the top of your neck upon skin from where
      fibers do not grow
Melt away your tension
Bring forth sighs
    groans
        closed eyes and
           fractions of daydreams

Suns

Wrap your hair around my hips in the same way the darkness
   drapes itself among the stars
Bringing the myriad of suns into view
Inspiring astronomers and poets to speculate about the reasons
   as to why
They fill our minds with wonder and
Our hearts with emotion.

Refusing

Her arms around me
    warm like a spring morning
The smell of her hair
My lips softly planted on a silky neck
Pressure of her breasts forced against my chest
    in our embrace
My hands lock behind her,
    refusing to let go

Satellite

Orbit around you, I do
Trapped by your gravity
Fixed, yet causing your oceans to pulse
Illuminating your night

Working

Leaves gently kiss the ground
The cool, dry morning air supplies a chill to the household
My lover accompanies me underneath my blanket
      on the sofa
Her cold legs and toes forcing tremors through mine
      robbing them of the heat they've retained
I laugh and wrap mine around her as a second, supplemental
      epidermal covering
She sits with me, enjoying the beating of my heart
The comforting scent of her coffee warms my senses
Laying her head back against my chest, she asks to hear what
      I am writing
I read aloud as she turns to me with eyes of approval
      and puckered lips of appreciation
A simple peck quiets her as she snuggles in, pulls the blanket
      to her chin, and enjoys me
      silently working

First

Water droplets fall from clouded skies
Relief to me comes in the belief that the rain may have fallen
     on you first

Stroll

Walk with me on this damp autumn evening
On my arm is where I need you
Leaves under our feet, harvest in the air
My softened heart is what you cling to

Childish stories of our younger years
In my ear I have your voice
Giggles, chuckles, smiles, and laughter
I don't think that there was ever a choice

The cool air blows your hair
Tickling the skin on my face
All I have and all I know is that
I never ever want to leave this place

Wonder

I wonder if at any point she rouses and thinks of me
Smiling before slipping back into unconsciousness

I wonder if she wakes with an aching between her legs
A pang that will not wait until dawn's early light

I have opened my eyes in the midnight hour with both

Flirty

The stars are a beloved sight
Their absence has left me lonely
I love to see their twinkles as if we're sharing a laugh or
       flirty wink

Release

She confessed things to him that he had never thought he
       would hear another human say
Words that constantly echo in his mind
Keeping him awake at night
Pulling on himself to satisfy his longest suppressed and
       self-ridiculed desires
So the warmth of validation could cascade over his hands
Setting him free

Stranger

Affix the blindfold over your eyes and
love me like a stranger

Meadow

Lie still
Let me feel you breathe with my mouth
      on your skin
Adorning you with hickeys and bite marks
The way the first blossoms of spring ornament a
      sleeping meadow

Off

She lies there with a racing heart
Unable to see as the lights were off and silently she knew
       his pants were too

Legato

The notes I long for my tongue to play
      between your open legs
Shall be an opus for the ages

Wash Over Me

Blinded and restrained on my back in my sleeping quarters
    she kisses me
        prying my mouth open with a
           determined tongue
Exploring my mouth with hers and my body with her hands
She delights in tickling me, bringing screams of
    painful laughter
She continues until I can hardly breathe

The kisses and hands return
I feel fear-laced excitement wash over me as a second
    set of hands wrap around my ankles
They slide up my legs
    then knees
        then thighs
    finding
        pulling and
           massaging me until I am engorged
           with blood
A softness indicative of a mouth surrounds me
I gasp into my lover's lips
    "shhhhhh" she whispers

Then all sensations cease

The rocking of the bed gives hints to the actions taking place
    over me

The movement
        the sounds
A finger laced with woman is forced into my mouth

The audible kissing
        sucking and
                slapping becomes deafening to my
                sight-deprived set of senses
Without my will to do so
        I shudder
                tense and
                        erupt across my abdomen to their
                        delightful amusement

A warm tongue and soft lips trace across my skin and devour
        the result of my imagination as a woman is
        lowered to my mouth
As I taste the inner circumference of her heated lust
        my tired
        flaccid
        cock is grabbed and strangled to a
        second
        throbbing
        painful erection where I am used again and again
Eventually they tire and I am left in the silent darkness
        of my bondage

What I would have given for a single glimpse

Cloak

The lengthening of the shadows
Sunlight becoming a warmer shade of amber with each
       passing moment
Air becoming cool and still
Silence slowly settles across the landscape as my
       true nature awakens to permeate bodies with lust
       and desire under the cover of nights darkening cloak

Restaurant

Standing from my chair I walk around the table to her
Patrons of the restaurant silenced to my ears by the
         desire in my mind
I invite her to stand and push her face town to the table
         gently lifting the fabric of her dress to gaze upon
         the beauty underneath

I slide a hand to join each leg beneath her undergarment
         up to where her torso is released
Turning my hands I make two fists, palms facing me
         the waistband of her panties within them
I bring them forcefully to her knees and encapsulate her
         womanhood with my hot, eager mouth
Exploring every portion of which she keeps private

She shyly makes eye contact with several of the shocked
         onlookers
This, causing a shuddering body to fill my mouth with the
         familiar taste of her fulfillment
Whimpering, she drops limp arms to the table top

All this in my thoughts between the moment we greet and the
         second she has a seat at the table

Voice of God

She comes to me like a child
Approaching the altar I am with caution and fear
A lack of understanding that keeps her within the
       threshold of conformity
I long to untie her by binding wrists and feet
       setting her free with restraint
Opening her eyes with the blindfold I use to cover them
The voice of God audible when I enclose her ears allowing
       her only to feel me
I penetrate every opening of her body
Physical sensations louder than thunder, brighter than staring
       into the midday sun
Blind and numb to everything except for the
Fullness from the relentless pounding
The pressure of my commanding grip and
The burning of her skin between my teeth

Signed

Lying together in the dark
  bodies glistening in what moonlight peeks through
    the windows
Running a finger from your chin
  down your clavicle
     back up and across your collarbone
As if I am placing my signature on the Pollack-like
  piece of art I've created

That's Mine

Pulling me into the coverage of the evergreens
Soft mitten-covered hands held to my face while open lips
        invite me in
The blending of the frigid air and her breath play games with
        the nerves around my teeth

She parts our lips
        smiles
                giggles
                        drops to her knees in the snow and
                                releases me through my zipper
"Right. Here." She says softly
She swallows me whole and I erect from the warmth of her
        mouth and the wrapping of her tongue around me

Achieving the desired reaction she stands
        lifts her long skirt and
        exposes her panty barren ass to me
Someone planned ahead
I slide into her with ease
Grabbing her waist and pumping furiously to not waste
        the heat our clothing had once kept against our skin
Cold air rushing around me with each stroke providing an
        amazing sensation against the backdrop of warmth
        bestowed to me from inside her body

A pale ass pinkening with exposure to the cold begs for
        attention

With one hand a hard slap is provided to the right cheek
The sting amplified by the ambient temperature of the
            winter air
Another and another
Her grip on me clinches with each strike
Reaching forward I toss the hat from her head
            grabbing a fistful of hair and
                        pulling her back
Softly spoken expletives and increased exhale fog from her
            darling lips let me know that now is not the time to stop
Harder contact is made with each thrust until she begs for
            me to hold inside of her
She tenses and twitches around me and I can take no more

Pulling out from her, my hot ejaculate puddles at the
            top of her ass
Slowly it finds the fjord separating her legs and is pulled
            lower with gravity

I stoop to rest the tip of my tongue on her clitoris and when
            the lukewarm fluid rolls across it into my mouth I move
Scooping between her lips
            across her plateau
                        slightly dipping the tip into her ass as I rise
                                    bringing all I've released into my mouth

She stands and proclaims
"That's mine!"
Before stealing it from me with her own delicious tongue
            swallowing it as we kiss

My pants are zipped
Her skirt flows back to her ankles and we continue our walk

through the park
The flush of our cheeks not apparent to those we pass
because of the cold

Tick Tock

Take me slowly
Inch by inch
Make the time painful

When I am completely inside
Make me wait

Have me close my eyes and forget
The stellar woman I've become one with
Before violently reminding me

Times

There are times she needs to be loved
Her hair softly placed behind her ears before the softest of
        kisses graces her forehead
Then there are times she needs to be thrown on the ground,
        clothes ripped off, and her body
            absolutely destroyed

Gleam

When she unbuckles my belt the gleam in her eye
      informs me that I am at her will
Loving greedily with her mouth
      it is apparent that she refuses to confine her exploring
            fingers to assisting with the task she has brought
               upon herself
She gags and giggles
      sighs and growls
Clutching her chest with a free hand as we enter and exit
      each other
Pressure
      palpitations
         release
           silence

Exchange

As the liquid component of my lust leaves me to find her
      cheeks, lips, and chin
She looks at me with the complete satisfaction of an
      accomplished artisan
The precipitation of warm fluid drips to her chest
While eyes close in the comfort of being
Marked
Branded
Owned by me
But behind my eyelids and heavy breaths I know that
      I have just given all of myself to her

Demons

Little red dresses summon my biggest, darkest demons

More Than One

Eyes wide open
      even though she's asleep
Secret wishes
      come to life in her dreams

Pushing herself
      to do all that she can
Simply begging to be
      taken apart by more than one man

Pale Into Pink

Further into depravity I sink
As each impact of my palm
Transforms the pale into pink

In Waves

Her soul begging for no less than
        the gripping of his fingers
                the impact of his palms
                        his teeth closing on her bare bottom to
                        commence the spilling of wine beneath
                        her flesh
Blue hues against pale skin like a still frame of the
        aurora borealis
Her body thanking him for the sensation
A nagging tenderness travels through her
        in waves
Ebbs and flows that roll through her being now that he is
        inside of her
Eyes blissfully clinch with every forceful meeting
        of their bodies
Persuading a kaleidoscope of color to dance across the inside
        of her eyelids
Until her body shivers
        quakes
                trembles and
                        she drops lifeless to the plush
                        bedding below
A tributary of fulfillment flowing from between her legs

Dark Light

When I am finished with your body
I want you subconsciously praying for forgiveness
      from a god you've never believed in
It is surely required as a result of the blasphemous
      sacrifices you have made at the altar of me
For the moment I held position in every possible
      opening at once
You saw a dark light that for a second made you
      fear for your soul

A New Goddess

Lips placed on reflective glass
      meeting themselves with closed eyes
Eyes she refuses to open the same way her mouth begins to
A soft tongue slowly appears to taste the silicate it is being
      pushed against
A frenzied hand grips a breast through her top
      eventually exposing both to the air with an
      impatient tug at her neckline
Nipples stiffen as each are
      squeezed
          twisted and
             rolled between thumbs and forefingers
A wandering hand finds its way between welcoming legs
She spins deepening circles until she begins to melt
      holding nearly her entire weight with the open mouth
        being forced against its now blurred reflection
As she blissfully blossoms onto the palm of her hand
      opening eyes become widened and stare
      into themselves
      finding a strange new beauty in their gaze

A new goddess revealed

Pleasure subsides and with fluid movements she steps away
    from the mirror
Admiring the abstract art comprised of
    exhale fog
        saliva and
            lip gloss
    before signing her work with wet fingers

Begging

The greed with which she sucked
Eyes full of hunger
Muffled sounds of satisfaction
      sending him elsewhere
To a place where he only saw her mouth feasting
      upon him
Her eyes taking in the sight of his empty face as he lay there
In a place where he could feel her eager hands
      wringing him
Where the only thing his ears could hear was the sound
      of her voice simply
           begging him to cum

Silently

Holding my hand
Silently looking into my eyes will reveal my soul
A heart that is
      gentle
           caring
                soft
Hiding a spirit that longs to love violently
Leaving aching
      sweat
           wobbling eyes
              physical exhaustion and
                  unexplainable fulfillment
Holding you in your recuperating slumber

Windsor

Two pulling motions release the tie from my shirt collar
Placing it between my teeth I approach her silently
        from behind
Hair between the point my lips meet her neck
Reaching between arms and torso I cup a clothed breast in
        each hand before squeezing and pulling her
           against me

Letting go my fingers find the highest button of her blouse
        releasing it
Working my way
        undoing each until nothing holds it together
I grab the back of her shirt collar and pull downward
        to release her

My right hand slides up her spine until the center of her bra
        is found
I push the loop end with my thumb while pulling
        the hooks with my first two fingers
A gentle "pop" releases the tension held by each clasp
I grasp between the cups and drag it away from her
        allowing her breasts to feel the coolness of the open air

Once dropped to the floor my hands interlock with hers and
        they are brought to hold the hair up from her neck

The tie is then taken from my mouth as the thin end is brought
        to the front of her chest and threaded between her
              neck and right shoulder

Slowly pulling the tie towards me I let every inch of it
            tease her nipple as she softly exhales
The thin end is woven through the space between the left side
        of her face and her shoulder
                laying against her chest
The spot my teeth held was rested against her neck providing a
        slightly cooled sensation where it meets her skin

I place her hands back to her sides
Holding each end of the tie
        I fold the larger half over the smaller
Pinching it with my left thumb and forefinger
Bringing the wide end under
        then back over
                encasing my forefinger
The slapping of the fabric tickles as it is brought underneath
        her chin
                causing skin to stand
She looks down and smiles as I slide the large end through the
        opening my finger was keeping for it
I complete the knot and slide it to rest comfortably at her neck

I step around to face her
Admiring the sight of the lengthy fabric laying between
        her breasts

"This is proper work attire." I say while straightening the
    windsor
"Now for an assignment I know you can excel at." is softly
    whispered into her ear before I grab the tie

       and pull her to her knees in front of me

Who Is

Grabbing your hair
Pulling your head back
Through your eyes into a soul I see
The question is such
"Who is my fucking slut?"
I hear you whisper "Please, let it be me."

Corruption

Everything she sees reminds her of him
    colors he wore
    something he said
The wind blows her hair and she wishes his hands were
    at her scalp
Gripping while caught up in an open-mouthed
    expression of adoration
Each time she sits she is reminded of the ferocity of his love
    by the gentle tenderness he left her with
Corruption of body and mind

Days

On days like these I need a woman
A walking
        talking
                feminine treasure
A conversation over lunch
To have her simply speak to me, reminding me
What it's like to be a man

Someone

The coolness of the pillowcase
Taken away by the breath that couldn't escape her
      open mouth
His fingers grasp the hair on the side of her head
      holding fast
      keeping her down
      rendering her immobile
His free roaming hand taking the rest of her body in its clutch
      sliding gently up and down her spine
Shock and surprise wash over her as an unexpected grip is
      placed on each side of her buttocks while
She is spread and entered by someone that
      she didn't know was in the room

Flavor

Above my chest you hold
Silent
Waiting
Feeling the pressure as he also enters
Curled lips and a wrinkled forehead lead to
Shocked eyes and a dropped jaw
While the commencement of our struggle for you
       as our possession begins
Competing for residence
Feeling one another through the thinnest of barriers
A grunt
An expletive
You fall to my chest
A sweet mouth that has forgotten to function
     allows saliva to fall and puddle
       slowly forced over my shoulder with your
       uncontrollable shuddering
Your weight changes with his every push
Differences in sensation that coax me to empty myself
     and he returns the favor
Sliding from underneath your smooth skin I turn
Placing my head between your legs
Joining me, we simultaneously devour where each had just
    finished
I feel you tasting yourself on my softening body
Each mouth saturated with the flavor of pure abandon and
Hell binding sin

No Vacancy

It was at that moment she wondered if she'd ever again be
satisfied with only one man inside of her

In Writing

Present to me in writing
The pre-assembled selection of syllables that you would like to
     be your shield
It is my very intention to test your every limitation as my lover
     tonight

King

Hovering over her as she shudders beneath me
I am on my throne and
      it is good to be king

Exorcise

I want nothing less than to be the reason you wake up
clutching yourself in the middle of the night
Tumbling into consciousness with demons to exorcise

So Much More

I will not beg
I will demand
You will provide
Understand?

On your knees
Hands on the floor
I want your whimpers
And oh, so much more

I slide my hand
Striking it fast
As much as you take is
How long this will last

I grip and I spread
Opening you wide
Placing my mouth
Tasting inside

Pushing, exploring
My hands and my tongue
Shudders and shaking
We've only begun

Spotless

Show yourself, my dear
Let me bathe you in my sight
Reveal to me all you wish to
So that I may provide compliments
      with the lathering of my vision
Rinsing you spotless as the liquid tendencies
      of my perception leave you
Cleansed and ready for the taking

Aching Pulse

When finished I want your
    legs weak
        knees shaking
            heart racing
                head spinning
Hands too feeble to hold the sheets and
Arms too tired to pull them if you could
Eyes drowsy
    lungs empty
        mind processing the sins we've just committed
So you simply lay there and feel the
    aching pulse
        where I was but moments before

Little Things

It's the little things she does
Winks
      pouting lips
          touching my mouth after touching herself
Handing me her panties under the table
Rubbing her back side against me while in line at the theatre
      draining me on the drive home

For Hours

Looking over her shoulder to see the assortment of implements
    she has assembled on the table
Beautiful choices
She presents me with the ball
    parts her lips
        turns and
            I slowly buckle it behind her
She sighs knowing that this is the only thing she will feel
    softly
For a moment I stare into her eager eyes
    scrutinizing
        studying
Letting her know that I am about to begin
    she nods
        murmurs and
            consents with a look of starvation
             developing between widely open eyelids
These eyes long to flow
    they long for release
    they long to have the pressures of the world
        taken from them

Without being asked for direction she lays a section of rope
    into my hands
The rope itself is beautiful
    smooth
        white
            Japanese silk

I take my sight away from the bundle in my hands to see her
          bent over
                    lying face down on the table
                              a gorgeous sacrifice on an
                                        altar of surrender
Loops are made around delicate wrists and each is anchored
          to it's corresponding table leg
Picking another section of silk, I kneel at her left ankle
          one loop
                    a second just above it
                              a knot
                                        and now she is attached to table
Steps are repeated for her equally beautiful right leg
I place my right cheek on the inside of her corresponding calf
          and slowly bring myself up
Dragging beard stubble up the entire length of the
          inside of her leg
                    stopping only to take in her scent
                              and taste the eager woman she is

I take steps back and admire her
          spread
                    vulnerable
                              breathtakingly bound body
Everything open and offered to me

I lift the plug and appreciate its weight
          a heavy
                    bulbous tool
Setting it down beside her I place closed lips on her anus
A soft meeting of lips to skin progresses to an ever more
          passionate kissing

My tongue probing
        pushing
                laying as much saliva into her as possible
Pulling my mouth away, I silently open a bottle of clear fluid
Holding it over her, I squeeze it slowly
        watching her twitch as the initial cold is a serious
                contrast to the heat that held her
                        moments before
The liquid cascades along her beautifully bound body before
        collecting in a small circle on the floor

Gliding my fingers across her sex brings a shimmer
        to the appendages
                which work their way up to where I was
                previously applying such
                passionate kisses
Hearing an exhale as I trace circles around her before
        my fingernail is no longer visible
                having disappeared inside of her
Slowly pushing in to the knuckle
        holding and repeating

A second finger is added
Both plunging
        pushing
                twisting
                        spreading inside of her until she is
                        relaxed and supple
My shimmering hand is removed and massages the plug
        until it too sparkles in the light
A transparent glass masterpiece is held against her

I apply more and more pressure before it disappears
    with her body wrapping around it
        while a low, guttural grunt is emitted
        from her throat
I give it a slap before stepping away from her

Picking up the flogger, I run the falls through my fingers
From where they meet the handle to the point that each end
    drops from my hands
Wrapping it around her face I let her take in the scent
    of the leather
Several breaths go by and I drag it over her left shoulder
    running it along the length of her spine
When the falls cascade over her legs a flick of the wrist
    throws them lightly back up to her ass
        providing the thud of their landing and
        a slight sting
Gentle flinging of the flogger turns into outright swinging
Her porcelain complexion pinkening with each impact

Moans and muffled screams present themselves with each
    subsequent strike

Thin, raised sections of skin slowly begin
    to present themselves among the
        pink and pale
Running my hands along the bare skin of her bottom
    allows me to read the story her flesh is telling
    from the way her welts meet my fingertips
        as Braille to a blind man
Kneeling in front of her, once again I study the eyes

Eyes that are full
    wobbling and
        ready to burst
An assertive nod lets me know that she is ready to progress

After a kiss to the forehead, I stand behind her with the
    end of the cane resting where her neck meets
    her shoulders
She feels the tip trace zigzags across her skin until I
    step to the side and begin tapping it where
    her legs meet her back
        over the curve of her beautiful ass
            down and stopping mid thigh
The heavy sting provides a burn that forces
    screams
        twitches
            sweat and tears to roll down her cheeks
Her body jumping
Slightly out of time with the quickening speed at which I
    bounce the implement off of her skin
Calves tensing but unable to lift themselves
Hands clenched in fists adorned with tight, white knuckles
Her muscular tensing crescendos and gives way to
    a silent, barely responsive third pass

After this pass I return my sight to her gaze

This time I see new eyes
Eyes that have let go of anything they've ever seen
The massive firing of nerve endings along with
    a flood of endorphins have set her free
The world has left her and she is where she belongs

A peace born from pain
    rebirth
    transcendence
    delivery
I speak softly to her and hear nothing but beautiful silence
Not even the sound of my voice rouses her

A soft towel is used to wipe the sweat and tears from
    her precious face
I swab gently over her entire torso
Wetting a second with warm water I tenderly dab along her
    bottom and legs
Along the violet skin that upon closer inspection is actually
    a tapestry comprised with shades of
        white, pink, and blue
Skin that allows traces of red to be absorbed into the fabric
    of the towel I use to clean her

Tossing the towel to the corner I concentrate on the
    untying of wrists
Gorgeous rings of white and red reminiscent of candy canes
    used to ornament the most festive of evergreens
Gliding my fingertips across the indentations left
    by her restraint is unnervingly satisfying
Hands are untied and continue to lay lifeless on the table top
Ankles are released from their binding and the nest of rope
    is tossed underneath the altar

Placing a thumb and forefinger around the end of the plug
    I twist and pull to the release of it from her body and
        a quick breath escapes her
Her admirable anus holds itself open for a few
    uncounted seconds before sleepily closing

It is placed on the table with a "knock" and the ball is
        unbuckled through the mess of sweaty hair on the
                back of her head

After helping her stand I adorn her porcelain shoulders with
        the softest of warm, cotton robes
Helping her push exhausted arms through the sleeves
I hold a glass of juice at her lips
        tipping it until the sugary fluid is taken in and
            after a swallow or two she blinks

Her eyes move and find mine
Followed by tears
      whimpering
          and arms that wrap tightly around my neck
She has come back to me
We embrace for what could have been an eternity as I feel
        her breathing and soft kisses pepper
          the skin of my neck
Slowly
One step at a time I guide a weary body to where it can rest
Laying her down, a blanket is draped over
        her astounding form
Hair is tucked behind her ears
Kisses are applied to cheeks and forehead as
      eyes close
         allowing her to rest

And as she does I watch her sleep for hours

Blink, Wish

A rush of wind
A blink of the eyes
Her heart makes a wish
That is carried to the skies

To feel the touch of his hands
Placed into and all over so many things
The dandelion seeds soon meet with the clouds
Lifted so high on the strength of dragonfly wings

Thank you.

Special thanks to all of the friends who have believed in, supported, and encouraged me along this journey. You are all amazing and your acceptance and kind words are never under appreciated. Thank you to Brooke for the initial proofread, to Alycia and Sara for the first peer read throughs, and to Alex at ABC Design for the fantastic cover art. Much love to all.

Made in the USA
Monee, IL
03 July 2024

61188347R00118